Animal Tales

Three stories in one

MICHAEL MORPURGO

EGMONT
We bring stories to life

Colly's Barn was first published in Great Britain 1991
Conker was first published in Great Britain 1987
Jo-Jo the Melon Donkey was first published in Great Britain 1995
Published in one volume as *Animal Tales* 2008
by Egmont UK Limited
239 Kensington High Street
London W8 6SA

ISBN 978 1 4052 3735 2

3 5 7 9 10 8 6 4

A CIP catalogue record for this title is available from the British Library

Printed and bound in UAE

Contents

Colly's Barn

Illustrated by **Ian Andrew**

MICHAEL MORPURGO

For Catherine, Simon, Jonathan,
Susannah and James
M.M.

To the memory of
Phil O'Connor
I.A.

Chapter One

SOMEONE HAD TO clean out the old barn. Grandad had a bad knee and her mother and father were busy, so Annie had to do it all by herself. But she wasn't alone. You were never quite alone in the old barn.

Screecher, the barn owl, looked down at her from his perch on the beam above her. She knew that the swallows would be watching her from their nests high on the roof joists. But the owls and the swallows were as much a part of the barn as the mud walls and the thatched roof and she paid them no attention.

It was hot work and smelly too, but Annie
was used to that. After all she had grown up
on a farm and on a farm there were always
smells of one kind or another. This was no
worse than most.

'Be nice if the cows would learn to clean up
after themselves,' said Grandad from the door

of the barn. 'I thought maybe you could do with some water.' They sat down side by side on a hay bale. Annie drank till the bottle was empty. Grandad was looking around him. 'This barn, your father wants to knock it down you know,' he said.

'What for?' said Annie.

'Old fashioned, he says, and maybe he's right.'
Grandad prodded the wall with his stick. 'Cob
that is, just mud, a few stones, straw; and it's
lasted all that time. Course there's a few cracks
in it here and there, but I told your father, it'll
go on for a few years yet.'

On the beam above them Screecher stretched his legs and flexed his talons. Grandad looked up. 'And Screecher, he's been here since the place was built, or his family has. Always nest in the same place they do. Same as those swallows, they've been coming here ever since I can remember.' Grandad stood up and leaned on his stick. 'Makes you think,' he said, 'thousands of miles they come every year, across African deserts, over the sea, and straight back to this barn. There's one now.' As he spoke Colly flew in over his head and up to the nest above, fluttered there for a moment and then swooped down again and out of the door.

'Look,' said Annie, 'there's a baby in the nest, you can see its head.'

'So you can,' said Grandad. 'You can hear it too. I wonder what it's saying.'

Annie laughed. 'Birds don't talk,' she said.

'Not like you maybe,' Grandad said, 'and not like me, but they talk all right. We just don't understand what they're saying, that's all. I wonder if they understand us?'

'Course not,' said Annie, but it gave her a lot to think about while she mucked out and when you've got something to think about time passes quickly. She never even noticed the evening coming on and she never once looked up at the swallows' nest again. If she had, she'd have seen the fledgling swallow perched precariously on the edge of its nest trying out its wings.

Screecher saw it but did not say anything. Colly was a good mother. She did not need any advice from him as to how to bring up her

family. She was his friend too, his oldest friend. They'd been living in the barn longer than any of the other birds. All winter, every winter, he would look forward to the day when Colly would come flying back into  the barn, bringing the spring with her. And when she arrived she never rested, not for a moment. She'd be building her nest, working every hour of the daylight. She'd hatch out her eggs and then she'd be flying in and out, in and out, keeping her family fed, and this year she'd had to feed them all on her own. No one really knew what had happened to her mate. He just went off hunting one morning and never came back. It could have been a car; it could have been a cat.

Screecher was just thinking about the cat when he heard her, and then he saw her creeping in through the door. Everyone warned everyone else. 'Look out! Look out!' they cried as the cat stalked stiffly past the hay bale and sat down under Colly's nest, her tail whisking to and fro, her eyes fixed on the nest above her.

Screecher knew what would happen, he'd seen it all too often before.

Suddenly terrified, Colly's last fledgling beat his wings frantically. Then he overbalanced and fell. The cat watched as he fluttered helplessly down towards the floor of the barn. She knew she had only to wait. There was no hurry, no hurry at all. She wasn't even hungry, she'd already had a nest of mice that day. This bird was for playing with.

At that moment Colly came gliding in, a mayfly in her beak. She dived at once, screaming at the cat, banked steeply and came in again. The cat ducked as Colly flashed by and she swiped the air with an unsheathed claw as she passed overhead. The fledgling was flapping his way to the corner of the barn. The cat crawled after him, belly on the ground, ignoring Colly's desperate attempts to drive her off.

There was only one thing Colly could do

now. She landed between the cat and her stranded fledgling and hopped away on a leg and a wing pretending to be wounded. 'I've broken it.' she cried. 'I've broken my wing.'

The cat stopped, turned and followed her. A big bird was always better sport than a small bird.

Screecher sprang off his perch and floated down on silent wings. The cat heard the whisper of wind through Screecher's feathers and looked up. She saw the spread white wings and the talons coming at her, open and deadly. She backed away in surprise. Screecher had never challenged her before.

'Colly,' said Screecher, keeping his eyes on the cat as she slunk away. 'I'm going to pick him up and put him back in the nest. Tell him to hold still. Tell him not to be frightened.'

His talons curled carefully under and around the fledgling. Then he took off, lifting him higher and higher until at last he was hovering above the nest and could let him go. The fledgling dropped down into the nest and huddled, complaining, in a corner. Colly landed beside him. 'I told you you weren't ready to fly yet, didn't I? I told him, Screecher. Wait till your wings are stronger, I said. Wait till tomorrow. But they don't listen.'

Screecher shivered. 'I think there's a storm coming,' he said. 'I can feel it in the wind. I'd best be off hunting before the rain comes,' and he opened his wings and lifted off the beam.

'Screecher,' Colly called after him. 'Thanks a million. I won't forget it, not ever.'

'What are friends for?' said Screecher as he floated away out through the barn door and into the dusk.

The road was always the best hunting ground. The hedgerows on either side were full of rustling voles and mice and rats. He had a good night of it. Five kills he made, but his two scrawny owlets just ate and asked for more. The rumble of thunder was coming dangerously close now. He'd been caught out in a storm once before. Once was enough. 'I'm telling you, you can't go hunting with wet feathers,' he told them, but that didn't stop them from grumbling on about how hungry they were.